RO

This

The
a fur

This book belongs to:

_____

_____

_____

For Mum and Lucy, who were kind to my caterpillars.
J. R.

For Mrs Moon's class — where beautiful little caterpillars
turn into beautiful big butterflies xxx
T. B.

Fletcher and the Caterpillar.
Published in Great Britain 2021 by
Graffeg Limited.

Written by Julia Rawlinson copyright © 2021.
Illustrated by Tiphanie Beeke copyright © 2021.
Designed and produced by Graffeg Limited
copyright © 2021.

Graffeg Limited, 24 Stradey Park Business
Centre, Mwrwg Road, Llangennech, Llanelli,
Carmarthenshire, SA14 8YP, Wales, UK.
Tel: 01554 824000. www.graffeg.com.

Julia Rawlinson is hereby identified as the author
of this work in accordance with section 77 of the
Copyrights, Designs and Patents Act 1988.

A CIP Catalogue record for this book is
available from the British Library.

ISBN 9781913733933

Teaching Resources:
www.graffeg.com/pages/teachers-resources

1 2 3 4 5 6 7 8 9

Fletcher and the Caterpillar

Julia Rawlinson & Tiphanie Beeke

GRAFFEG

The trees were stretching in the sun, their branches bright
with raindrops. Buds were swelling. Petals were unfurling.
Everything in the wood was growing… except one juicy
green leaf which seemed to be getting smaller. Fletcher
peered underneath the leaf…

...and found a tiny,
stripy caterpillar.

"Hello, Caterpillar," said Fletcher.

"Munch,"

said Caterpillar.

"Do you want to play?" asked Fletcher.

"Munch,"

said Caterpillar.

"What do you like doing?" asked Fletcher.

"Munch,"

said Caterpillar.

"Who are you talking to?" asked Squirrel, bouncing droplets from the branches.

"A caterpillar," said Fletcher, sheltering it with his paw.
"Do caterpillars like racing?" asked Squirrel, dashing up and down.
"Let's find out," said Fletcher. "Ready… steady… go!"

Squirrel raced up the tree.
Caterpillar munched.
Squirrel skittered down again.
Caterpillar munched.
"I don't think Caterpillar
likes racing," said Fletcher.
"Maybe the mice will know what
caterpillars like to do."

The mice were weaving willow boats
on the flowery bank of the stream.

"I've found a caterpillar," said Fletcher,
"but I don't know what it likes to do."

"Maybe it would like a boat," said the mice,
weaving leaves.

They made the boat a tiny mast out of a blade of grass and held it out to Caterpillar, who...

...munch, munch, munched.

"I'm sorry," said Fletcher. "I think it thought it was lunch."

Fletcher carried Caterpillar along the stream,
through the wood. They found the rabbits
playing hide and seek under the curling ferns.

"Caterpillar can hide," they said.
"We'll close our eyes and count to ten."

Fletcher tucked Caterpillar under a dripping fern.

The rabbits looked...

and looked...

and looked...

and flopped wearily down.
"Caterpillar's too small to find," they said.
"We need a different game."

But Fletcher was beginning to think Caterpillar didn't want to play.
Caterpillar just liked munching in a friendly sort of way.
Caterpillar munched while Fletcher paddled in the stream.

Caterpillar munched while Fletcher watched the drifting clouds.

Caterpillar munched while Fletcher sniffed the spring flowers.

Fletcher went to sleep and woke to
the sound of steady munching.
And then, one day…

...there was silence.

"Caterpillar has stopped eating," said Fletcher.
"Don't worry, they do that," said Mum.

"Caterpillar has stopped moving," gulped Fletcher.
"Don't worry, they do that," said Mum.

But Fletcher *was* worried.

He nestled his caterpillar in a bed of leaves and
watched over it as the sun set over the sleepy
wood. He watched over it as bats began to flit
between the shadowy trees. He watched over
it as the first stars brightened in the dusky sky.
And then, at last, he slept.

But through the quiet of the night,
Caterpillar wiggled, making a cosy chrysalis
home. So when Fletcher blinked awake and
peeped into the bed of leaves...

…all he could see was a little green blob.

"Caterpillar's turned into a blob!" cried Fletcher.
"Don't worry, caterpillars do that," said Mum.

"But you'll soon have something just as wonderful.
Wait and see."

So Fletcher waited patiently
through the endless days.
The gurgling stream slowed to a
trickle, the rich earth
turned to dust and the leaves
hung heavy on the trees.

Then one lazy afternoon, as
Fletcher dozed in the heat,
the blob began to stir.

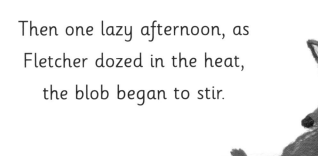

It gave a little rustle.

It gave a little wriggle
and out burst...

...Butterfly!

It crawled onto Fletcher's paw, stretched its shimmering wings and launched unsteadily towards the sun's bright blaze.

"I'll miss you," called Fletcher, but Butterfly flew back to him and led him through the golden wood in a twirling butterfly dance.

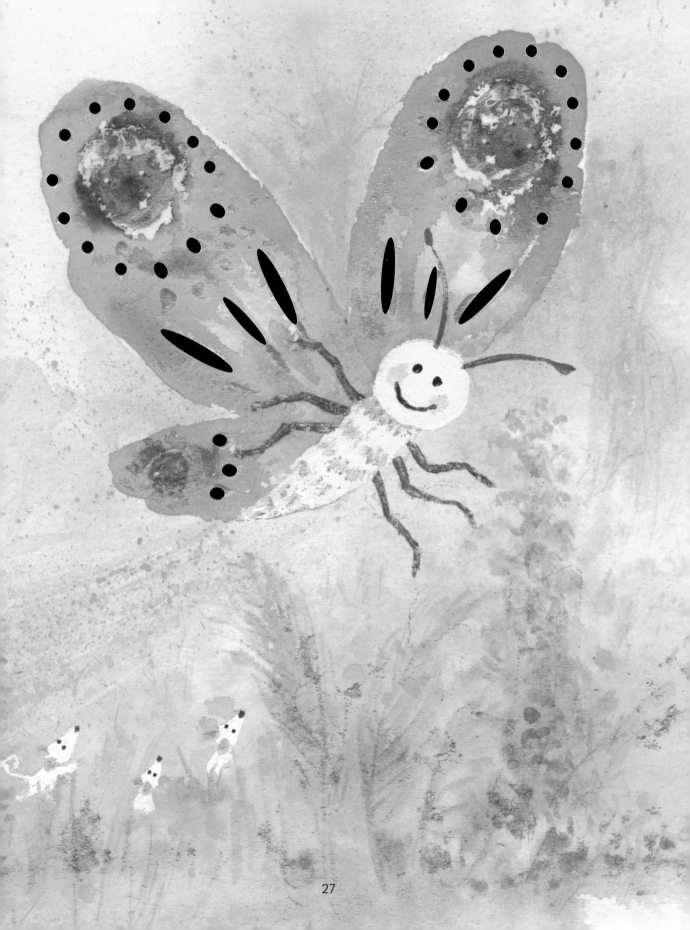

Fletcher Books

Discover the delights of the seasons in these exquisite and uplifting picture books.

ISBN 9781913134624

ISBN 9781913134631

ISBN 9781913134648

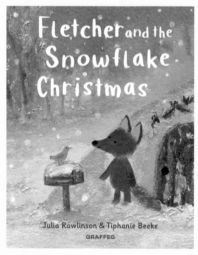

ISBN 9781913134655

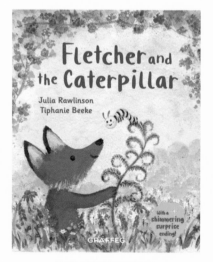

ISBN 9781913733933

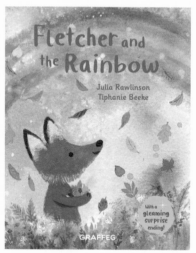

ISBN 9781914079245

www.graffeg.com

GRAFFEG